It's the coolest school in space!

Young Teggs Stegosaur is a pupil at
Astrosaurs ACADEMY – where dinosaurs
train to be space-exploring Astrosaurs.
With his best friends Blink and Dutch
beside him, amazing adventures and
far-out fun are never far away!

For more astro-fun visit the website
www.astrosaursacademy.co.uk

Find out more at www.astrosaurs.co.uk

Astrosaurs ACADEMY

STEVE COLE

JUNGLE HORROR!

Illustrated by Woody Fox

RED FOX

JUNGLE HORROR!
A RED FOX BOOK 978 1 862 30559 5

First published in Great Britain by Red Fox,
an imprint of Random House Children's Publishers UK
A Random House Group Company

This edition published 2009

5 7 9 10 8 6

The Random House Group Limited supports The Forest Stewardship
Council® (FSC®), the leading international forest-certification organisation.
Our books carrying the FSC label are printed on FSC®-certified paper.
FSC is the only forest-certification scheme supported by the leading
environmental organisations, including Greenpeace. Our
paper procurement policy can be found at
www.randomhouse.co.uk/environment

MIX
Paper from
responsible sources
FSC® C016897

Set in16/20pt Bembo Schoolbook by
Falcon Oast Graphic Art Ltd

Red Fox Books are published by Random House Children's Publishers UK,
61–63 Uxbridge Road, London W5 5SA

www.randomhousechildrens.co.uk
www.randomhouse.co.uk

Addresses for companies within The Random House Group Limited can
be found at: www.randomhouse.co.uk/offices.htm

THE RANDOM HOUSE GROUP Limited Reg. No. 954009

A CIP catalogue record for this book is available from
the British Library.

Printed in the UK by Clays Ltd, St Ives plc

For Joshua Wynn

WELCOME TO THE COOLEST SCHOOL IN SPACE . . .

Most people think that dinosaurs are extinct. Most people believe that these weird and wondrous reptiles were wiped out when a massive space rock smashed into the Earth, 65 million years ago.

HA! What do *they* know? The dinosaurs were way cleverer than anyone thought . . .

This is what *really* happened: they saw that big lump of space rock coming, and when it became clear that dino-life could not survive such a terrible crash, the dinosaurs all took off in huge, dung-powered spaceships before the rock hit.

They set their sights on the stars and left the Earth, never to return . . .

Now, 65 million years later, both plant-eaters and meat-eaters have built massive empires in space. But the carnivores are never happy unless  they're causing trouble. That's why the Dinosaur Space Service needs herbivore heroes to defend the Vegetarian Sector. Such heroes have a special name. They are called ASTROSAURS.

But you can't change from a dinosaur to an astrosaur overnight. It takes years of training on the special planet of Astro Prime in a *very* special place . . . the Astrosaurs Academy! It's a sensational space school where manic missions and incredible adventures are the only subjects! The academy's doors are always open, but only to the bravest, boldest dinosaurs . . .

And to YOU!

NOTE: One of the most famous astrosaurs of all is Captain Teggs Stegosaur. This staggering stegosaurus is the star of many stories . . . But before he became a spaceship captain, he was a cadet at Astrosaurs Academy. These are the adventures of the young Teggs and his friends — adventures that made him the dinosaur he is today!

Talking Dinosaur!

How to say the prehistoric names in
JUNGLE HORROR!

STEGOSAUR – *STEG-oh-SORE*

DIPLODOCUS – *di-PLOH-de-kus*

DICERATOPS – *dye-SERRA-tops*

ANKYLOSAUR – *an-KILE-oh-SORE*

DRYOSAURUS – *DRY-oh-SORE-us*

SEGNOSAURUS – *SEG-noh-SORE-us*

TRICERATOPS – *try-SERRA-tops*

PTEROSAUR – *teh-roh-SORE*

APATOSAURUS – *ah-PAT-oh-SORE-us*

SAUROPELTA – *SORE-oh-PEL-ta*

SEISMOSAURUS – *SIZE-moh-SORE-us*

IGUANODON – *ig-WA-noh-don*

BRONTOSAURUS – *bron-toh-SORE-us*

LAMBEOSAUR – *LAMB-ee-oh-SORE*

KOTASAURUS – *KOH-toh-SORE-us*

The cadets

THE DARING DINOS

Teggs   Dutch   Blink

DAMONA'S DARLINGS

Damona   Netta   Splatt

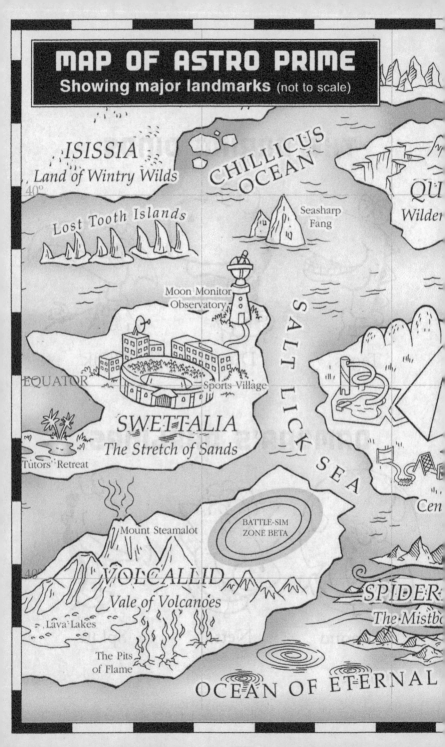

Chapter One

ALARM IN THE NIGHT

Teggs Stegosaur was having a fantastic dream.

In the dream, he was whizzing about in a space-tank, firing dung-balls at an army of attacking T. rexes. "Take that, short-arms!" Teggs growled, splatting one gruesome monster right in the eye. "Mess with me and you'll be stung by my dung!"

But then a loud, insistent bell went off, *DING-A-LING-A-LING-A-LING-A-LING!*

The dream-world vanished as Teggs jerked awake in his bed in the dino-dorm. For a moment, he was sorry his action-packed dream had ended. Then he remembered that he was a cadet at Astrosaurs Academy, training to join the Dinosaur Space Service, ready for a lifetime of adventure! And that really is a dream come true, Teggs thought happily.

The noisy alarm wasn't stopping,
*DING-A-LING-A-LING-A-LING-A-
LING-A-LING!*

Frowning, Teggs switched on his
bedside lamp and turned to his two
roommates. Blink, a yellow dino-bird
with a beak like a
giant banana,
yawned and
stretched his
wings. Dutch,
a short green
diplodocus,
was gently
snoring
through the
racket.

"Guys!" Teggs
shouted. "I don't
know whose alarm clock that is, but
switch it off!"

Suddenly, Blink somersaulted out of
bed in a panic. "That's no alarm clock!"

3

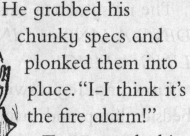

He grabbed his chunky specs and plonked them into place. "I-I think it's the fire alarm!"

Teggs caught his breath. "You're right." Now he was wide-awake he could hear that the ringing was coming from *outside* their dino-dorm. "When the fire bell goes, everyone is meant to line up on the athletics track outside the academy."

"Let's see if we can be the first ones out," said Blink. "It might mean extra points for our team!"

Teggs nodded eagerly. All the cadets had split into teams on their first day at Astrosaurs Academy, and he and his friends had called themselves the Daring Dinos. It was a name they had lived up to during several wild adventures, and

Teggs's tummy tingled at the thought of a new adventure just beginning.

Blink hopped onto Dutch's back and danced up and down. "Wake up!"

"I'm asleep, dude," Dutch groaned. "What's with all the bells?" But the next moment he leaped out of bed, sending Blink squawking through the air. "Hey, I can smell smoke! Is someone having a barbecue?"

"We wish . . ." Teggs ran to the window and opened the curtains. Some way away he could see flames dancing in the darkness.

"Looks like this fire alarm's for real – and I think the Daring Dinos should be in on the action." He turned to his roommates and held out his hand. "Do we dare?"

Dutch and Blink put their hands on his. "WE DARE!" they all yelled.

Teggs beamed and dived out through the dino-dorm window, landing softly on the blue grass outside. Dutch tumbled after him, while Blink launched into flight.

"I'll see what's happening from up above!" the pterosaur called.

"Let us know," Teggs shouted back, as he and Dutch galloped across the grass towards the floodlit athletics track in their pyjamas.

They overtook lots of dinosaurs but they weren't the first cadets there. Damona Furst – a red diceratops with two horns, six freckles and an attitude problem – was already standing on the track. Beside her stood a feisty, pink ankylosaur called Netta, and Splatt, a lean, green dryosaur. Together they were Damona's Darlings – the Daring Dinos' biggest rivals.

"What took you so long, boys?" said Damona, raising her eyebrows.

Splatt grinned. "Yeah, we've been waiting here for ages."

"You just missed the robo-hoses whizzing by," Netta added. "What a sight!"

"Typical," grumped Dutch. He and Teggs could see the fire more clearly now, blazing around a large dome to the north of the Central Pyramid. Dozens of robo-hoses – emergency water-carrying robots – were already tackling the flames with their aqua-jets.

"Looks like the fire broke out in the teachers' block." Teggs looked round at the crowds of cadets gathering on the track, and realized there were no teachers among them. "I hope everyone got out to safety."

"Blink will be able to tell us," said Dutch.

Just then, an astro-jet rose up into the flame-filled sky from beyond the teachers' buildings. It turned and soared away into the night.

Damona frowned. "I wonder who's on board that thing?"

"All right, cadets!" came a throaty voice behind them. "Stop gawking and pay attention!"

Teggs and his friends whirled round to find a large, female segnosaurus. Her red astrosaur uniform clashed with her scaly violet skin. She looked grave as she held up her long claws for silence.

"Well done for lining up so quickly,"
said the segnosaurus. "My name is
Commodore Kallos."

"She's got a good reputation," Damona murmured. "My Uncle Hiro fought with her, years ago."

"Now, you may all go back to bed," Kallos announced. "Everything's under control."

Teggs saluted. "Excuse me, Commodore, but did all our teachers get out of the block safely?"

"They weren't even *in* the block, cadet." Kallos smiled. "Just a few hours ago, my old buddy Commander Gruff called a special secret conference for his staff over on Junglus."

"Where?" Dutch asked.

"It's the land of jungles in the east, you dummy," said Damona. "The Savage Safari Park is there."

"That's where they hold the annual Splatter-Gun Paintballing Championship," Teggs recalled. "I've always wanted to go there!"

"Now, while Gruff and his gang are away, I'm in charge," Kallos went on. "I've got ten supply teachers coming. You will meet them in the morning."

A thought struck Teggs. "But if all the teachers are in Junglus, who just left in that astro-jet?"

"The caretaker," Kallos explained. "He started the fire by accident, trying to fix a broken fuse. He seems fine, but I'm flying him to hospital in Swettalia to get him checked out just in case."

"That's all right then," said Netta.

Splatt nodded. "Let's get back to bed!"

As the cadets started to plod across

the lawn to their rooms, Blink swooped down and landed next to Teggs and Dutch. He was sooty and out of breath.

Damona smirked. "Trust beak-features to miss everything."

"That astro-jet only just missed *me* as it took off!" Blink said. "I didn't see it for all the smoke at first. Commander Gruff was on board, I hope he's OK."

"Don't talk rubbish," said Netta. "Gruff's in Junglus. The new acting principal just said so."

"What?" Blink frowned, blinking like

crazy. "But I'm *sure* I saw him!"

"It was the caretaker, dude," said Dutch, yawning. "The heat must've steamed up your glasses."

Teggs felt a pang of unease. It wasn't like Blink to get his facts wrong. But then a high-ranking astrosaur would hardly lie to them. Would she?

He glanced over at Commodore Kallos. She was watching him closely with the faintest of smiles on her face . . .

Chapter Two

LOUSY LESSONS

The next morning, Teggs, Blink and Dutch hurried into the learning halls for their navigation class. They were last to arrive.

A small, stern-looking triceratops sat in the teacher's chair. "I am Sergeant Palo," he said. "And *you* are late! Just sit down and click on Sector Seven in your star charts because today we will be studying the planets in the Geldos Cluster."

"Er, but that's not *in* Sector Seven, sir," chirped Blink. "It's in Sector Twelve."

Palo gave Blink a stern look. "It's in Sector Seven, cadet. Look at your star chart."

Teggs sat at his ultra-desk between Blink and Dutch and clicked on the chart of Sector Seven. Sure enough, the Geldos Cluster flashed into view.

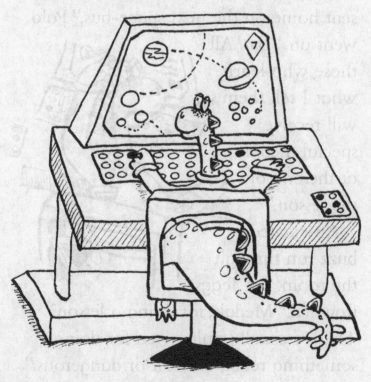

Blink did the same, then blinked in puzzlement. "Perhaps there's a computer fault, sir? Only I was studying these charts in my nest the other day, and I'm certain—"

"Are you calling me a liar, cadet?" roared Palo.

Blink gulped. "N-n-n-n-no!"

"Anyone who causes trouble will be sent home on the next space-bus," Palo went on. "*But!* All those who learn what I tell them will receive special medals at the end of the lesson."

An excited buzz ran through the room, but Teggs frowned. "Medals, for doing a lesson? They're usually only given for doing something really difficult or dangerous."

"Don't knock it, dude!" said Dutch, grinning.

"The Geldos Cluster is in Sector Seven – sorted!" Netta declared.

Splatt nodded eagerly. "What do we have to learn next?"

Blink sighed and worked on quietly with a down-turned beak. At the end of the class, when Palo handed out shiny silver medals to all the cadets, the dino-bird took his award politely and pushed it straight into his pocket.

"What's up?" Teggs asked.

"I don't think I earned my medal," said Blink. "I thought I knew a lot about space, but those charts have shown me I'm completely wrong!"

The pterosaur waddled sadly away.

Dutch put his own medal round his neck and frowned. "Blink always comes top in navigation class. It's not like the little dude to be wrong."

"He was wrong about seeing Gruff last night," Damona reminded him.

"I suppose he was," Teggs agreed, looking thoughtfully at the shiny medal in his hand.

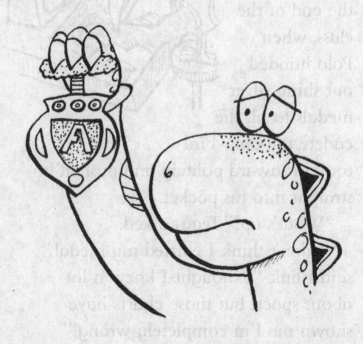

At lunch time, Teggs and Dutch cheered up Blink by treating him to a crunchy bug cocktail. Then it was straight off to space-tank class – Teggs's favourite lesson!

Their usual instructor had been replaced by a purple apatosaurus called Prox.

"Today I will show you how to load long-range dung-bullets into your tank-guns," Prox announced. "Turn to page seven of your new textbooks and study the plans."

Teggs looked and shook his head. "But, sir . . . these plans are all wrong!"

Prox scowled. "Think you're an expert, do you?"

"I've read a hundred books about space-tanks," said Teggs proudly. "I've got two hundred models. I even dream about them!"

"Well, this is a super-secret, cool new design," Prox told the class. "I wanted to give you cadets the honour of being the first to study it. But if this young stegosaur makes any more trouble, we will look at the boring out-of-date plans instead."

"No!" cried Damona. "Shut up, Teggs."

"We want to learn how to use the new version," agreed Akk, a smart black sauropelta.

Blushing, Teggs kept silent for the rest of the lesson. Now he knew how Blink had felt.

"Good work," said Prox as the cadets filed out. "I will give a special silver medal to anyone who can memorize those plans by next week's lesson."

"Awesome!" Dutch declared. "These new teachers are cool."

Splatt nodded keenly. "We'll have tons of medals in no time!"

"Attention, cadets!" Commodore Kallos's voice rattled over the academy loudspeakers. "Please gather outside the Central Pyramid for a special message from Commander Gruff."

"Come on, guys!" said Teggs. "Let's hear it!"

With Blink and Dutch, he hurried
through the crowded corridors towards
the main exit. A huge TV screen stood
outside the pyramid, already surrounded
by a crowd of onlookers. Suddenly, the
familiar figure of Commander Gruff –
a grizzled seismosaurus, with an unripe
banana clamped between his lips
like a cigar – appeared in front of a
banner marked WELCOME TO THE
SAVAGE SAFARI PARK. He was sweating
a lot . . . clearly it was hot over in
Junglus.

"See, Blink?" Netta nudged him in the
ribs. "You *can't* have seen Gruff on that
astro-jet!"

"Greetings, cadets," their head teacher
began slowly. "I wanted you to know . . ."
He hesitated, then took a deep breath
before he continued. "I called the urgent
meeting of my staff here in Junglus
because I think the time has come for
me to retire."

Teggs Blink and Dutch gasped, along with most of the startled crowd.

"That's not all," Gruff went on. "My teachers fancy a change too, and have decided to leave with me. So, I am handing over the running of Astrosaurs Academy to Commodore Kallos and her crew while the rest of us enjoy a holiday here in the Savage Safari Park." He smiled suddenly. "I hope that you will give your new teachers the support they deserve. See you around, troops." Teggs had the strange feeling that Gruff was looking straight at him. "Make me proud, you hear?"

The screen switched off.

"I don't believe it!" Blink whispered.

"I'll miss that scuffed-up old scowler," Dutch murmured.

Then an armoured dino-car rolled up carrying Commodore Kallos. She was grinning broadly and waving to the crowds. "You heard old Gruff! I'm your new principal," she cried. "There will be a big feast in the canteen tonight so we can celebrate ... and I'll award a special medal for whoever eats the most puddings!"

Her news was greeted with hearty cheers. Dutch joined in, licking his chops. But for once, Teggs didn't feel hungry.

"It looks like Astrosaurs Academy is under new management," said Blink nervously. "Whether we like it or not!"

Chapter Three

TEACHER TROUBLE

Teggs went along to the big party with
Blink and Dutch and did his best to
have a good time. He ate twenty-three
helpings of fern pie. He boogied with
Blink. He cheered when
Dutch came first in
the pudding-eating
contest. But he
couldn't stop
thinking about
Commander Gruff's
surprise announcement.

"If Gruff's retiring, why
aren't we having a party for *him*?" he
wondered aloud.

"You're just grumpy because you got told off by one of the new teachers," teased Damona, munching on some space-biscuits.

Perhaps I am, thought Teggs. Perhaps tomorrow will be a better day.

But Teggs found that the next day was even worse.

In astro-history the cadets were handed textbooks that contradicted things they had already been taught.

"Your old textbooks were wrong," said this instructor. "My new ones are correct. And if you learn all the facts properly you will each get five medals!"

"*Five?*" Teggs spluttered.

"Awesome!" cried Splatt.

Straight after that was strategy class, where new teacher Major Gator insisted that the best strategy in a space battle was to make lots of nutty decisions to confuse your enemy.

"If your opponent can't guess your next move, how can he beat you?" said Gator.

"But he won't *need* to beat us!" Dutch argued. "He'll just zip straight past us while we're mucking around."

"Is that so?" Gator glared at him. "Good cadets get chocolate ferns to eat in class — but *you* can stand at the back."

Dutch watched, drooling, as everyone else ate their tasty treats. Blink and Teggs tried to save him a couple of mouthfuls but Gator made them eat every last crumb.

"I'm not missing out on a free snack again," Dutch declared at the end of the lesson. "Next time I'll just shut up and get on with it."

"No, Dutch, you were *right* to speak out," said Blink. "Our old teachers taught us to think for ourselves. These new ones don't want us to question *anything*."

"Well, I think it's better this way," said Netta, overhearing them. "If we keep quiet they give us treats and medals. It's easy."

"Maybe *too* easy." Damona sighed. "I

love getting awards – but if you get one for doing nothing, it *means* nothing."

"Careful, Damona," laughed Splatt. "You sound like Beak-brain!"

"*You* sound like someone with a sore foot," Blink retorted – and pecked Splatt on the toe!

"*Ow!*" Splatt hopped away on one foot. Dutch high-fived Blink, and even Damona and Netta had to laugh.

The day ended with a PE class for Teggs and Dutch, while Blink went off to space-geography with Damona's Darlings.

"Not even these new teachers can mess up a game of astro-rugby," said Teggs happily as the final whistle ended sixty minutes of nonstop muddy action. "I wish I could run as fast as you, Dutch."

Dutch shrugged. "I wish I could smash through a scrum the way you can!"

As they headed for the showers with

the other players, Teggs suddenly noticed a scowling red figure stomping across the pitch. "It's Damona!"

"Hey, dude," Dutch called. "What's up?"

"That geography teacher knows *nothing*!" growled Damona, marching up to them. "My great-aunt discovered the ruby planet of Raxas Four in the Outer Fringes, sixty years ago – right? But according to her precious new textbook, there's no such planet!" Damona pulled the book from her bag and waved it angrily. "Of course, I argued – and got sent outside for the rest of the lesson. *Me!* Sent out!" She chucked the textbook onto the ground in disgust, and a small slip of paper fell out.

Teggs picked it up and frowned. "This is funny," he said. "It's a delivery note. This book was one of three hundred delivered to the Savage Safari Park in Junglus." He scratched his head. "Why would anyone deliver academy textbooks to a safari park?"

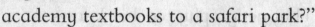

"That's where Commander Gruff and the others have gone, isn't it?" Damona stamped her foot crossly. "Oh, I wish we could talk to old Gruff! He might change his mind about retiring if he knows how Commodore Kallos and her team are running things."

"I had the same idea!" With a flap of leathery wings, Blink swooped down beside them, out of breath. "After yet another lousy lesson, I decided to phone the Savage Safari Park and talk to Commander Gruff. But no one answered."

"Maybe the staff were having a tea break," Dutch suggested.

"Maybe," Blink agreed. "But, listen – remember how I thought I saw Gruff on that astro-jet leaving the teachers' block?"

Dutch nodded. "Kallos said it was taking the caretaker to hospital in Swettalia."

"Well, when I couldn't get through to

the safari park, I decided to call the hospital and check the caretaker was OK," Blink went on. "And guess what the doctors said . . . ? No astro-jet ever arrived there, and no caretaker was taken for treatment."

Teggs gasped. "So Kallos was lying!"

"And that astro-jet went somewhere else," Damona realized. "Maybe Gruff *was* on board — with the other teachers. Maybe they were *forced* to go to Junglus."

"And Gruff was forced to give us that message," Blink agreed.

"No wonder Kallos and her gang don't want us to question things," said Teggs gravely. "If we're right, it means that Gruff's been kidnapped and Astrosaurs Academy is in the hands of the enemy. We've got to do something — and fast!"

Chapter Four

FLIGHT INTO DANGER

"So what's our plan?" asked Dutch.

"We must find Gruff as quickly as possible." Teggs turned to Damona. "You're always saying what a fabulous pilot you are. If we borrowed an astro-jet, could you steer it to Junglus?"

"Of course I could. You know me — I'm extra-special and super-brilliant!" She grinned. "I'll tell Netta and Splatt what we're planning."

"Er, I don't think you should," said Blink. "The fewer people who know, the better."

"Besides, Netta and Splatt *love* the new teachers," Teggs reminded her. "They might try to stop us talking to Gruff!"

"I suppose so." Damona sighed. "Well, at least they won't get into trouble if we're completely wrong."

"I hope we *are* wrong!" Teggs admitted. "Let's meet at the astro-jet launch pads at midnight. The sooner we slip away and sort this, the better!"

At midnight, Teggs, Dutch and Damona

crept cautiously up to the launch pads. Blink flew silently overhead, checking for security guards.

"Just one," he whispered as he landed. "An iguanodon, over by the satellite tower. It'll take him about five minutes to get here."

Teggs looked at Damona. "Can you get us airborne in five minutes?"

She frowned. "I'm not sure."

"Well, now's your chance to find out!" He looked at Dutch. "Shall we?"

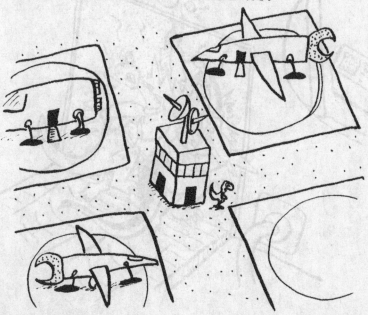

Dutch nodded – then, he and Teggs charged at the doors of the nearest astro-jet. With a grinding squeal the metal doors crunched open enough for them to squeeze through. At once, alarms blared and bright-red warning lights flashed on and off all around them.

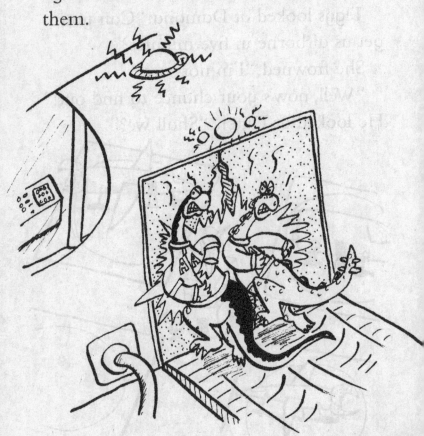

"Everyone in!" Teggs hollered.

Damona was first on board, racing through to the control room with Blink just behind her. She flicked several switches and started up the engines.

While the sirens wailed on, Teggs and Dutch patched up the doors they had just bashed in as best they could, then joined their friends.

"One minute left," Teggs reported.

Damona nodded, settling into the pilot's seat. "Beak-brain, turn off the auto-locks on the wheels – that lever there!"

Blink whacked it with his wing. "Done."

"Thirty seconds left!" cried Teggs.

The sound of gunfire started up from outside. "Uh-oh," Dutch said, peering through a window. "More guards – with lasers! The doors won't last ten seconds against those ..."

"Taking us up!" shouted Damona, grabbing the flight stick and pressing on a big blue pedal as the engines roared like twenty T. rexes in torment. The astro-jet lurched away, knocking Teggs and Dutch to the floor.

"You did it, Damona!" Teggs cheered.

"Just *keep* doing it," Dutch urged her.

Blink was already peering at a map.
"I'll work out the fastest route to the
Savage Safari Park. At least we'll have a
head start on anyone trying to follow."

The astro-jet flew out over the deep,
orange ocean. Minutes passed in a tense
and slightly air-sick silence.

Then, a loud beep came from the communicator, followed by a familiar husky voice. "This is Commodore Kallos calling Teggs, Damona, Blink and Dutch. Security cameras caught you leaving your dorms and heading for the launch pads. Return that ship at once!"

"Um, we can't, dude," said Dutch. "See, we're learner drivers and we can't remember how to steer."

"Don't play the fool, cadet!" Kallos snapped. "Commander Gruff will be very upset with you. He told you to treat me

and my staff
with the respect
we deserve."

"Exactly,"
Damona
retorted.

"And you
don't deserve *any*
respect for kidnapping all our teachers
and trying to take over the academy."

"Too right!" Teggs agreed.

There was a long silence.

"So," Kallos hissed at last, "you know
that we are agents of the Carnivore
Crime Cartel, here to fill your heads
with false information and useless battle
strategies!"

All four cadets gasped.

"Er, actually we didn't," Teggs
admitted. "But thanks for sharing."

"What a crafty scheme," muttered Blink. "We are the astrosaurs of the future. It stands to reason that if the meat-munchers mess up our training, we will be useless at defending the Vegetarian Sector from carnivore attacks."

"Well, your plan won't work, Commodore Kallos," said Damona fiercely. "Because we are going to rescue Commander Gruff from the Savage Safari Park and when he gets back he'll kick you out of the academy for sure."

"You will never get there, cadets," Kallos assured them. "I'll see to that."

"Oh, yeah?" said Teggs defiantly.

"Well, Gruff told us in that message to make him proud, and that's what we're going to do." He switched off the communicator and sighed. "At least, I hope we are!"

Dutch smiled and held out his hand. "Do we dare?"

Teggs and Blink put their own hands on top of his. "WE DARE!" they chorused.

"And so do I!" added Damona. "On behalf of my own team, naturally."

But then Blink started twittering. "Oh, no! Look at the radar screen. Two more astro-jets are coming after us!"

"We're going at top speed," Damona told him. "They can't outrun us."

"But they *can* launch their missiles at us!" cried Dutch as two more small dots suddenly appeared on the screen.

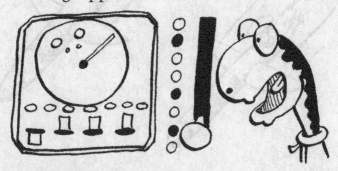

"Quickly! Change course!" Teggs snapped.

Damona yanked on the flight stick and the ship veered sharply to the  left. But the dots moved instantly to follow the ship's new bearing.

"They're guided missiles!" groaned Blink.

"And they're gaining on us." Dutch swallowed hard. "In a couple of minutes we'll be blown out of the sky!"

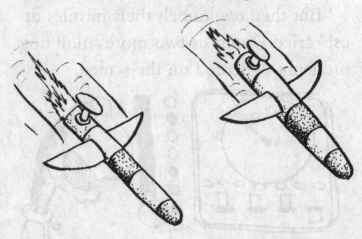

Chapter Five

MAYHEM IN THE AIR

"We've got just one chance!" cried
Teggs. "Damona, keep our course
straight. Dutch, come with me." He
charged back down the corridor to the
damaged doorway and kicked one of
the doors. It rocked alarmingly.

"Are you crazy, dude?" Dutch yelled.
"We're two miles above the ocean and
those doors are still loose. If you open
them you'll get sucked out of the ship!"

"Not if you hold onto my tail very tightly," Teggs told him with a crooked smile. "Brace yourself. I've got to time this exactly right . . ."

"Those missiles are almost on top of us!" Blink wailed from the control room.

"Here goes!" Teggs hurled himself at the dodgy door and grabbed it by the handles as it was snatched away into the dark, freezing sky. But Dutch kept a tight grip on his tail, flying Teggs like a spiky, seven-ton kite, gasping with the effort.

Still clutching the door, Teggs could see the two menacing missiles side-by-side, streaking out of the darkness towards their jet. He let go of the door and it went spinning away . . . .

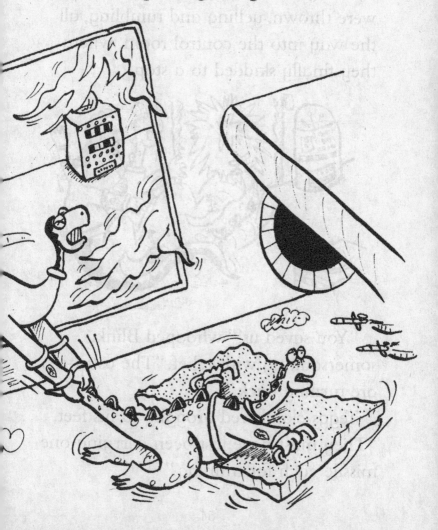

Right into the path of the missiles!

The sky turned red with an enormous explosion. The shock waves sent Teggs flying back through the doorway and crashing into Dutch. The two of them were thrown, yelling and tumbling, all the way into the control room, where they finally skidded to a stop.

"You saved us!" whooped Blink, somersaulting with relief. "The astro-jets are turning back."

Teggs clambered groggily to his feet. "They must have just been carrying one missile each for training."

"But those shock waves have damaged the engines," cried Damona as the astro-jet started to wobble alarmingly. "We must land as soon as we can."

"Look!" said Dutch weakly, his head squashed up against a window. "There's a beach in the distance. Must be the coast of Junglus, right?"

Suddenly, the communicator beeped again. "You were lucky this time, cadets," Kallos rasped. "But your luck is about to run out!"

The communicator went dead.

"What do you think she meant by that?" wondered Damona.

Teggs looked grim. "I have a nasty feeling we're going to find out very soon!"

★★★

Far across the ocean, snug in his dino-dorm, Splatt woke with a start – the fire alarm was going off *again*!

Grumbling, he quickly dressed and raced outside, zipping between the crowds of cadets as they headed for the floodlit sports track. Netta was already waiting there – alone. "Where's Damona?" he asked.

Netta shrugged. "I don't know. When I woke up, she wasn't in her bed."

"Wait."

Splatt cocked his head to one side, listening. "What's that roaring noise . . . ?"

The next moment, three high-speed dino-carriers swooped overhead. Cadets scrambled out of the way as the gigantic ships came into land in a thick cloud of smoke.

The door of the largest ship opened to reveal Commodore Kallos. "Attention!" she boomed. "*I* set off the fire alarm to wake you up – because I am sending you all on a special training mission called 'Hunt the Spies'."

She pressed a button on a small gadget, and the images of four faces were projected into the sky. Splatt gasped in astonishment.

"That's Damona!" Netta spluttered. "And Teggs and his team."

"To make the mission extra-real, the cadets you see here are pretending to be spies," Kallos went on. "An orange-brown stegosaurus, a red diceratops, a dark-green diplodocus and a yellow pterosaur. Remember those details. All four 'spies' are hiding in the jungles of Junglus – and you must hunt them down."

"She must have chosen them because they argued with teachers," Splatt whispered. "I'm glad we kept quiet!"

"To prove you have found them, you must slosh each of them with one of these . . ." She held up a chunky metal weapon. "It is a special splatter-gun that fires balls of paint.

Anyone who manages to splatter a spy will be awarded twenty-three special medals and a month off from all lessons!"

Netta's eyes widened. "Imagine that!"

Splatt grinned dreamily. "I am!"

"Now, get aboard the dino-carriers, cadets, and help yourselves to splatter-guns," Kallos shouted. "It's time this hunt got started!"

Cheering wildly, the cadets surged forward and piled into the ships — ready for their most exciting mission yet!

"Hang on, everyone!" Damona called to her passengers, steering the shaking astro-jet over the beach. "This is going to be bumpy!"

Teggs, Blink and Dutch grabbed hold of each other as the ship skimmed the orange waves and smashed into the sand. They yelled, sent flying as the astro-jet flipped over and bounced back into the air before falling with a spine-crunching, ear-splitting *crash*. Damona nodded approvingly. "Better than my last landing!"

"Good work," said Teggs, rising on wobbly legs. "Now, let's get going."

Before they could move, the communicator bleeped again. "I just wanted to warn you to start running," said Commodore Kallos, mockingly. "I've sent three hundred cadets after you on a training exercise. They think you are pretending to be spies, and their mission is to slosh you with splatter-guns."

"So they shoot paint at us and stain our uniforms," said Damona. "Big deal!"

"Ah, but what your friends don't know is that the paintballs they're firing have a special added ingredient . . ." Kallos chuckled. "They contain an explosive powder that will *blow up* as soon as it hits a living creature. The moment your friends hit you, you will go up in smoke!"

Blink's beak went white with shock. "You won't get away with this!"

"It's your class-mates who will take the blame, not me," she retorted. "And if the Dinosaur Space Service asks, I'll simply put it down to some dodgy guns and call it a tragic accident! Boo-hoo . . . Or rather, *HA! HA!*"

As Kallos cackled away, Teggs

switched off the communicator and turned to his frightened friends. "We must move out, right now!"

"Wait," hissed Blink. "What's that noise?"

They listened with growing horror to the distant hum of engines approaching over the crashing orange waves.

"It's them!" Damona cried. "Three hundred cadets with orders to slosh us on sight. We don't stand a chance!"

Chapter Six

THE HUNT BEGINS!

"Come on!" cried Teggs, leaping down
from the astro-jet onto a patch of beach
at the rainforest's edge. "We've got to
get away from here!"

In the dawn light, he looked around
for a likely path through the
towering trees blocking
their way.

Grey mist swirled eerily about the
spindly trunks and fat, fleshy leaves,
and the noises of jungle birds
and beasts filled
the air.

"Wow!" said Dutch, jumping down beside Teggs and tucking into a bush. "This place is like a buffet waiting to happen."

"I know!" Teggs grabbed a mouthful of creepers.

"Dense jungle like this will give us good cover from flying paintballs," Blink noted. "Provided you two don't eat it all, of course!"

"Let's get going," said Damona, as the sound of the approaching astro-jets grew louder. She marched up to the jungle edge – then gasped as a terrifying creature burst out of the bushes before her! It had the face of a giant crocodile and the body of a grizzly bear.

With a howl of hunger it raised its terrible claws to strike Damona . . .

But then Blink bravely flapped up into the croco-bear's face. The beast swiped at him — giving Teggs and Dutch the chance to sock it in the stomach with their powerful tails.

Beaten back and gurgling crossly, the croco-bear lumbered away into the jungle.

"Thanks," said Damona shakily.

"Maybe we can find a safer path into the jungle further down the beach," Teggs suggested.

"No time!" Blink squawked as two huge shadows fell over the beach. "The cadets are coming!"

Three huge dino-carriers slowed to a stop high above the coastland stretch, small, dinosaur-shaped specks already spilling from the sides and inflating their parachutes. Over the noise of engines, Teggs could hear excited whoops and shouts: "*Look! A red diceratops, an orange-brown stegosaurus, a dark-green diplodocus and a yellow dino-bird. That's them — our targets!*"

"Time to split," said Dutch.

"Wait!" called Damona, shielding her eyes against the glare of the morning sun. "I can see Netta and Splatt. They'll help us." She started jumping up and down. "Hey, you two!"

"Hi, guys!" Netta waved as she floated down towards the beach, clutching her splatter-gun. "Or should I say, 'Hi, *spies!*'"

"Look out!" Damona knocked Teggs aside as Splatt and Netta opened fire. The paint splattered harmlessly against a nearby tree.

"Stop shooting!" Teggs bellowed up at them. "This isn't a game."

"Kallos is a carnivore agent!" Damona added. "We're trying to get to

Commander Gruff so he can put things right."

"I never knew you lot were so good at acting!" Splatt grinned. "You're saying all the things a spy would say to try to put us off. But it won't work!"

Netta opened fire again, and so did Splatt. Soon the other parachuting cadets were firing too, each of them frantic to tag the spies and claim the glory.

"Damona, guys — into the jungle!" Teggs bellowed. "*NOW!*"

Blink, Dutch and Damona sprinted after him as the beach about them erupted in sticky, multicoloured explosions. Soon they were running for their lives through

the hot, misty gloom of the rainforest.
They stumbled over tree roots, bundled
through bushes, splashed through
steaming puddles and
skidded through
smelly white
mud. A stitch
burned in
Teggs's side,
but he didn't
dare stop.
Behind him
he could hear
the telltale
crash and
clatter of dozens
of dinosaur cadets,
hard on their heels.

"What can we do?" Blink twittered.
"Just one hit and we've had it!"

"Let's split up," said Teggs. "I'll try to
lead the cadets away while the rest of
you head for the Savage Safari Park.

Blink can guide you from the treetops."

Dutch shook his head. "I'm faster than you, dude, remember? *I'll* lead the cadets away."

"I'll go with you," said Damona. "Splatt and Netta are my team-mates – they might just listen to me."

Teggs sighed and nodded. "Good luck!"

"See you soon," added Blink hopefully.

Dutch and Damona charged away as quickly and noisily as they could, while Teggs and Blink quietly sneaked off in the other direction. Gradually, the sounds of pursuit died away.

"It worked!" Blink hissed. "The cadets must think we all stayed together." He hopped onto a large, blood-red flower and tutted. "Oh, I do hope Dutch and Damona are— *URK!*"

"You hope they're '*Urk*'?" said Teggs, only half-listening. Then he realized

Blink was no longer beside him and whirled round – to find the petals of the flower had snapped shut around Blink, trapping him inside!

"Help!" Blink gasped. "This plant wants to eat me!"

Teggs swung his spiky tail like a pickaxe and chopped through the flower's thick stem. Green goo gushed everywhere, and Blink burst out from the rubbery petals like a magician's dove from a red silk hanky.

"Are you OK?" asked Teggs anxiously.

"F-f-f-fine." Blink shivered, panting for breath. "Come on, let's go. Whatever the dangers, we *must* get to Gruff quickly – before it's too late!"

Chapter Seven

THE SAVAGE SWAMP

"Come on, dude," Dutch panted, dragging Damona clear of a thick patch of thorns. "We can't stop now!"

The two desperate dinosaurs ran on through the steaming jungle, soaked with sweat and covered in scratches. So far they had managed to stay ahead of the excited cadets chasing them.

But they both felt themselves slowing down. The jungle vines seemed to have a life of their own, tangling around their ankles. Hissing snakes tried to chomp their tails and giant flowers with billowing petals sucked at their skin.

Suddenly, Damona skidded to a stop. "Careful, Dutch – looks like a swamp ahead."

Dutch stared at the stretch of squelchy, watery mud and sighed. "We'll have to go around it."

"No time," hissed Damona. The sound of rustling bushes and breaking branches was growing ever louder behind them.

She pointed to a wide, black rock in the middle of the swamp. "We can use that as a stepping stone."

Dutch took a deep breath and leaped through the air. He landed safely on the rock. But all of a sudden, it shifted beneath him – and a giant slimy head burst out of the mucky water close by! It was smothered in lots of red eyes and sharp teeth, swaying on the end of a gigantic neck.

Damona stared in horror. "Jump, Dutch!" she yelled. "That's no rock – it's the back of a giant swamp-monster!"

"Now she tells me," he groaned. The swamp-monster opened its spiky jaws and tried to bite him, but Dutch dived clear just in time. Unfortunately he fell straight in the water with a splash and got tangled up in sticky pondweed. "I'm stuck!" he cried as the swamp-monster reared over him, licking its many lips with twelve revolting tongues. "Get out of here, Damona, there's nothing you can do!"

At the same moment, a green figure burst from the undergrowth behind Damona. She whirled round to find herself face to face with Splatt!

"Found you first!" Splatt cried triumphantly, and raised his gun. Then he saw the hideous swamp-monster towering above Dutch and jumped backwards in shock. "W-w-what is *that*?"

"It's about to eat Dutch – what more do you need to know?" Damona shouted. "Use your splatter-gun."

He stared at her. "That's no good, it only fires paint."

"That's what *you* think." Damona snatched the gun, aimed at the big, green beast and fired. The paintball sloshed against its back – and exploded! With a roar of anger and pain, the smarting swamp-monster sank beneath the steaming surface to soothe its scorched hide.

"Thanks!" called Dutch gratefully, finally pulling himself free of the pondweed.

Splatt looked at the gun in amazement. "One paintball did *that*?"

"Kallos has mixed the paint with an explosive powder," Damona told him. "She knows we're trying to rescue Gruff, so she sent you, and every other cadet, to stop us."

"Rescue Gruff?" he repeated, blankly.

"He hasn't retired, he's been kidnapped!" Dutch staggered out of the swamp, coated in brown mud. "Kidnapped by Kallos and her crew."

Splatt gulped. "*Seriously?*"

Damona gave him back his gun. "If just one paintball hits us, you'll have all the proof you need!"

Splatt stared down at the splatter-gun. Then he shuddered, hurled it into the swamp and gave Damona a quick hug. "We must hide you somewhere safe."

She shook her head. "Until Gruff is back in charge, nowhere is safe! We've got to help Teggs and Blink rescue him from the Savage Safari Park."

"But this whole jungle is full of cadets out to get us!" Dutch sighed. "What can we do?"

"For a start, *you* can have a wash!" said Damona, holding her nose. "Look at the state of you!"

"Hang on!" A smile had edged onto Splat's face. "You've just given me a fantastic idea ..."

After a hair-raising, skin-prickling, sweat-soaked hour spent crawling, tiptoeing and flapping through the jungle, Teggs and Blink had finally reached their target. The large banner welcoming visitors to the Savage Safari Park looked identical to the one they'd seen in Gruff's video message. A burly ankylosaur guard blocked the winding, grassy path that led inside.

"How do we get past him?" Blink whispered.

"For once, this *nutty* rainforest is on our side," said Teggs, pointing to a bunch of yellow coconuts dangling above the guard. He whacked the trunk with his tail, and the coconuts rained down like missiles. Conked twice on the head, the guard slumped to the ground.

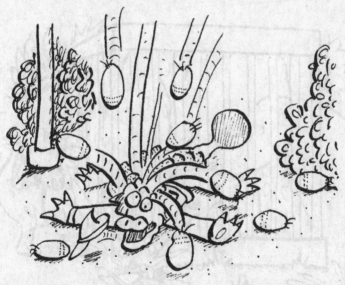

"In we go!" Teggs charged past the sleeping guard and Blink flapped along beside him. The path soon twisted sharply to the left, revealing a large metal cage.

A gigantic green figure lay squashed up inside. His eyes were closed and a battered banana dangled from his dry, cracked lips . . .

"Oh, no," breathed Teggs, his heart sinking. "We've found Commander Gruff — but too late to save him!"

Chapter Eight

SHOWDOWN!

Teggs and Blink took a step closer to the commander's cage. Then suddenly, the giant green body shifted and Gruff opened his eyes. "I'm not finished yet, cadets!" he growled, forcing a smile.

Teggs swapped a relieved look with Blink and saluted. "You had us worried there, sir!"

"Kallos still needs me alive to sign some special forms that will put her in charge of Astrosaurs Academy for ever," Gruff explained. "As soon as they arrive from the DSS and she has my signature, she can get rid of me." He flipped the bruised banana back into his mouth and winked. "You got here in the nick of time, boys. Glad you showed up!"

"I'll try to crack this electronic lock, sir," said Blink, pecking at a small computer panel on the cage door with his beak. "If I can only reset the automatic timer . . ."

"Where are the other teachers, Commander?" asked Teggs.

"Kallos has locked us all in different cages. She's as cunning as they come. I've known her for years, but I never dreamed she was a secret agent of the Carnivore Crime Cartel!" Gruff sighed. "She and her team smuggled themselves into the Savage Safari Park weeks ago in crates marked "WILDLIFE". Then they jumped out, surprised the staff and managed to take control."

"That explains why those bogus textbooks were delivered here," Teggs realized. "Straight into her hands!"

"My staff and I played straight into her hands too." Gruff sighed. "Kallos started a fire in the teachers' block, and when we rushed outside, her agents knocked us out, dragged us onto an astro-jet and took us away."

"So much for her story about the caretaker!" Blink looked up from the lock excitedly. "I *knew* I'd seen you on board!"

"Now Kallos has told the DSS that I asked her to come and take over," Gruff went on. "She told me that if I didn't announce my sudden retirement, she would feed my teachers to the croco-bears – then squish all the cadets!"

"It's a good thing you *did* send that message, sir," said Teggs. "It proved you were here, so we knew where to find you—"

"Just as *I* knew exactly where to find *YOU*!"

The familiar voice jolted through Teggs and a violet figure appeared from behind the cage. "Commodore Kallos!"

"Run, cadets!" Gruff barked. "That's an order."

"Shut it, you has-been!" Kallos pressed a button on the side of his cage and Blink jumped clear as thick, soundproofed steel walls slid down,

blocking the commander from view.
Then Kallos's fake-teacher friends –
Prox, Palo, Major Gator and all the
others – followed her out of hiding,
surrounding Teggs and Blink in a
threatening circle.

Kallos smiled coldly. "Since all the cadets are out hunting for you, my instructors have no one to teach. So I decided they could come here with me, to deal with you in case you tried to escape . . ."

Just then, Teggs heard pounding footsteps on the grassy path, drawing closer. For a moment his heart soared, imagining Dutch and Damona racing to the rescue. But his hopes fell like a one-legged brontosaurus on stilts . . . The newcomers were a grey triceratops, a small, dark-brown diplodocus in a filthy uniform – and Netta!

"*FOUND YOU!*" Netta bellowed, pushing through the ring of teachers and raising her gun.

"Excellent work, cadets." Kallos clapped her clawed hands together. "Go ahead and slosh them."

"Don't, Netta!" cried Blink. "If you do, you'll kill us!"

"Kallos is a traitor." Teggs pointed frantically to the shielded cage. "She's got Gruff bundled up in there!"

"*As if!*" snorted the triceratops, bursting out laughing. Netta and the diplodocus joined in. The fake teachers started chuckling too.

"You expect us to believe a story like

that?" Suddenly,
Netta stopped
laughing. "OK,
then — because
it sounds like
the same story
Splatt told me!"
With that, she
swung her club-
like tail and
knocked Kallos's
legs out from
under her.

At the same
time, the triceratops lowered her head
and charged into Prox and Palo. The
diplodocus moved too, lashing out with
his long tail and toppling Major Gator.
He pointed his splatter-gun at the
confused teachers still standing.
"Nobody move!"

Teggs gasped in amazement. "That
voice . . ."

"It sounds like Dutch!" trilled Blink.

"That's because it *is*, dudes!" The smiling diplodocus wiped his dirty face to reveal familiar green skin beneath. "I've just gone undercover with a little muddy make-up."

"And so have I!" The triceratops yanked off her nose-horn and tossed it to Teggs – who realized it was simply a fir cone covered in mud.

He and Blink both realized at the same moment: "*Damona!*"

She fluttered her muddy eyelids. "The one and only!"

"It was Splatt's idea," said Netta breathlessly. "He got the lowdown on Kallos from Damona and Dutch, then came and told me."

Dutch nodded. "And since the hunt was on for a red diceratops and a green diplodocus, Splatt and Netta disguised us so we could move around without being sloshed!"

"Brilliant!" Teggs grinned. "Where is Splatt, anyway?"

"It doesn't matter," snarled Kallos, scrambling back up. "Because your clever little trick has got you nowhere."

"Stand still." Netta waved her splatter-gun. "You, of all people, know what this paint can do."

"Exactly." Kallos smiled. "Which is
why my allies and I put on special body
cream this morning that protects us
from its effects – just in case some over-
excited cadet got trigger-happy."

"You're lying," said Damona,
uncertainly.

"The cream contains tiny plastic
particles that defuse the explosive
charge. Watch!" Kallos snatched the gun
from Netta and fired at Major Gator.
Teggs gasped in horror – but the yellow

paint sloshed harmlessly over the major's legs.

"You see?" Kallos hissed triumphantly. "What a pity you have no such protection." She pointed the weapon at Teggs, ready to fire. "The hunt is over, cadets – and *I* am victorious!"

Chapter Nine

THE LAST LESSON

"Not so fast, dude," Dutch blurted, still wielding his splatter-gun. "There *is* a way these weapons can hurt you."

"There is not," Kallos insisted.

"Is too!" Dutch clonked her on the head with it, and she staggered backwards. "See?"

"*RUN!*" yelled Teggs, leading the others away from the cage up a steep hillside, desperate to escape Kallos's line of fire. Already the paintballs were flying around them. If just one of them hit . . .

Teggs dived over the top of the hill to escape the storm of paint and tumbled down the other side. His friends rolled alongside him. But, as they jumped back to their feet, all five of them froze.

Ahead of them was an enormous jungle lake, filled with dirty orange water.

"Not fair!" Damona stamped her foot in frustration. "If we try to swim across, we'll be easy targets."

"You already are," crowed Kallos from the top of the hill. With her teacher chums behind her, she swaggered down towards the helpless cadets. "And once you're out of the way, no one can stop my plans."

"Don't underestimate the cadets of Astrosaurs Academy," Teggs shouted back.

"Those fools?" Kallos scoffed. "They will do anything for a few treats and medals. By the time they leave the academy, their heads will be dizzy with my false facts and silly strategies. They'll be helpless before the cruel might of the carnivore forces!" She raised her gun.

"Now, prepare to be sloshed!"

Teggs stiffened. "Er, there's still one thing I don't understand."

"Well, I'm supposed to be a teacher . . ." Kallos sniggered. "Ask away!"

"Why did you bother to turn ordinary paintballs into deadly weapons?" he called.

"Because it's impossible to sneak real weapons past the academy's security satellites," Kallos told him. "I knew I would need them to deal with Gruff and his staff, and troublesome twits like you . . . and since there were already hundreds of splatter-guns here for the cadets to use in their training, my masters simply sent me a crate of chemicals I could mix into the paint to make an explosive powder."

"And is that how you started the fire in the teachers' block before you kidnapped Gruff and our teachers?" asked Blink loudly. "With your exploding paintballs?"

"Naturally!" She snorted with laughter. "Anything else you'd like to know before I blast you to bits?"

"Just one last, tiny thing . . ." Teggs grinned broadly, pointing behind her

with his tail. "Now that you've just confessed to your crimes in front of three hundred armed and very cross cadets, what are you going to do next?"

"*What?*" Horror-struck, Kallos and her team spun round . . . to find scores of sweaty, angry students with splatter-guns, glaring down at them from the top of the hillside!

"Morning, all!" Splatt pushed forward to the front of their ranks. "Hope you don't mind extra company, but I led them here!" He smiled. "You know, not all of them believed me when I told them what you were up to – but now they've heard the truth from your own dumb mouth!"

"I . . . I was just joking!" Kallos began nervously. "It's all part of the training exercise!"

"Shut up!" growled a lambeosaur. "You tricked us."

"You wanted *us* to do your dirty work," cried a kotasaurus. "You took away our teachers and you tried to hurt our friends."

An angry iguanodon nodded. "You sent us here to Junglus to catch some spies – and that's just what we're going to do!"

"Never!" Kallos screamed. "Not when my crew and I can swim away to fight another day!" With that, she and the other carnivore agents pushed past Teggs and his friends and hurtled into the lake with a colossal splash. They started swimming for the other side with all their might.

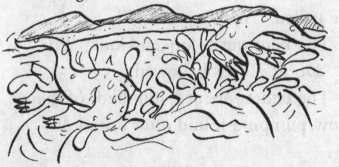

Splatt led the angry cadets down the hillside to the water's edge. "Stop, or we fire!"

"Go ahead!" sneered Kallos. "Our special protective body-cream just happens to be waterproof too!"

Damona groaned. "They're safe from the paint. We'll have to swim after them."

"No, wait – maybe we don't *have* to hit them . . ." Teggs turned to the gathered army of cadets. "Fire into the water ahead of Kallos and her gang!" he yelled. "And *keep* firing!"

The kotasaurus looked blank. "Eh?"

"Do it!" Teggs bellowed.

The cadets obeyed, hundreds of them now, pumping round after round of coloured paint into the dirty orange lake. Dutch joined in, though he looked doubtful. "What good will this do?"

"Wait and see . . ." Blink was nodding his head and blinking furiously. "Yes! Yes, Teggs, it's working!"

Even from a distance, it was clear that Kallos and her cronies were finding it harder to keep on swimming. The water around them was already thick with paint, and getting sludgier all the time as more and more of the stuff plopped down like multicoloured rain. The villains' limbs moved more and more slowly through the paint-storm. Soon, most of them could hardly move at all.

With a yell of
helpless fury,
Kallos finally
realized she
wasn't going
anywhere and
raised her hands
in surrender. An

enormous cheer went up from the
cadets, who started hugging and high-
fiving each other.

"All right, cadets, simmer down," came a familiar growling voice. "We've got a lot of clearing up to do."

Teggs whirled round in amazement. "Commander Gruff!" he gasped. "You're free!"

Gruff grinned down at Blink. "All your fiddling with that automatic timer paid off, son. Five minutes after the shutters came down, they bounced back up and the door sprang open."

"Really?" Blink turned a twittery somersault. "Woo-hoo! I did it!"

"Awesome!" Dutch yelled, grabbing his friends in a big, muddy embrace as Commodore Kallos hung her head in defeat.

"Cadets," Gruff boomed, "I hear you've been given a lot of meaningless medals lately." He smiled at Teggs. "Well, as a result of their actions here today, I shall be giving the Order of the Noble Nanosaur to two titanic teams – the Daring Dinos and Damona's Darlings!"

Blink gulped. "That's one of the highest honours an astrosaur cadet can earn."

"And boy, did we earn it!" said Splatt, laughing as another huge cheer went up from the assembled dinosaurs.

"The rest of you will also get a special reward for your part in today's victory," Gruff went on. "A whole rocking week of *safe* paintballing here at the Savage Safari Park!"

Again the cheers went up, but Gruff waved his tail for silence. "Now, stay here and guard those bad guys. I must radio for a rescue ship and some robo-hoses to suck all that pollution out of the lake. But first, I'm going to unlock the rest of your teachers . . ."

Netta watched him go and grinned cheekily. "No rush!"

"Speak for yourself!" said Blink. "I can't wait till things are back to normal again."

"Yup," Dutch agreed. "This is the best school in the universe."

"With the best ever students," Damona added.

Splatt nodded. "And the best ever friends."

"*And* the best ever adventures!" Teggs grinned. "I hope we're going to stick together through the years and have many, many more . . ." He held out his hand. "Do we dare?"

The others happily piled in to put their hand on his, and all yelled together, "*WE DARE!*"

THE END

The cadets will return in . . .

DEADLY DRAMA!